THE
BALLOT BOX BATTLE

Emily Arnold McCully

Alfred A. Knopf ❦ *New York*

THIS IS A BORZOI BOOK PUBLISHED BY ALFRED A. KNOPF, INC.

Copyright © 1996 by Emily Arnold McCully
All rights reserved under International and Pan-American Copyright Conventions.
Published in the United States by Alfred A. Knopf, Inc., New York, and simultaneously in Canada by
Random House of Canada Limited, Toronto. Distributed by Random House, Inc., New York.

http://www.randomhouse.com/

Printed in the United States of America

Library of Congress Cataloging-in-Publication Data
McCully, Emily Arnold.
The ballot box battle / by Emily Arnold McCully.
p.   cm.
1. Stanton, Elizabeth Cady, 1815–1902—Juvenile literature.
2. Feminists—United States—Biography—Juvenile literature.
3. Suffragists—United States—Biography—Juvenile literature.
4. Women—Suffrage—United States—History—Juvenile literature.
I. Title.
HQ1413.S67M34   1996
324.6'23'092—dc20   95-38095
ISBN 0-679-87938-2 (trade) —0-679-97938-7 (lib. bdg.)

10 9 8 7 6 5 4 3 2 1

To Madeline and Anna

With thanks to Paula

*A*ll the summer of 1880, Cordelia's job was to go next door, feed Mrs. Stanton's horse, and clean out the stall. Every afternoon, Mrs. Stanton put aside her work on *The History of Woman Suffrage* and gave Cordelia a riding lesson. When she talked about some skirmish in her long battle for the vote, Cordelia always minded her manners and pretended to pay attention, but it seemed to have nothing to do with her. Riding was what she cared about.

By autumn, Cordelia could trot, canter, gallop, and jump over a low crossbar. When she bragged to her brother, Howard, that she could ride, he said, "Oh, well, you are not a true horseman until you jump a four-foot fence."

She repeated this to Mrs. Stanton. The great lady sighed. "I'm afraid old Jule is too worn out to jump that high. But someday you will have your own horse and you will do it."

Cordelia was disappointed. She wanted more than anything to jump a four-foot fence now. After their lesson on the first Tuesday in November, she asked, "Mrs. Stanton, did you jump when you were my age?"

Mrs. Stanton didn't answer at first. "Do you know that today is Election Day, Cordelia?"

Cordelia shook her head no.

"A new President will be chosen. But no woman will vote," Mrs. Stanton went on.

Well, why should they? Cordelia thought. *All that was done by men.* She repeated her question. "Mrs. Stanton, did you jump a four-foot fence when you were my age?"

Mrs. Stanton said, "Indeed, I jumped a four-foot fence and across a ditch. I did it to prove my courage."

"Why?" Cordelia asked, very interested.

"There were six children in my family. The only boy was my older brother, Eleazur. He was the pride of my father's heart, a new honors graduate of Union College. Suddenly, dear Eleazur fell ill. Then he died."

Cordelia gasped. What if Howard were to die?

"We were all so sad. But my father's spirit was utterly broken. Every day and nearly all night, he sat in the darkened parlor beside Eleazur's coffin.

"For me, it was as if I were losing Father, too. I couldn't bear it. So I went into the parlor and climbed onto his lap to comfort him. He didn't speak for a long time. Finally, he said, 'Oh, my daughter, I wish you were a boy!'"

"Oh, my," Cordelia whispered. She wondered if her father wished she were a boy, like Howard. Were boys really better than girls? "What did you do?"

"I said, 'Papa, I will try to be all my brother was.'"

"But how?" Cordelia asked.

"On the spot, I made a resolution to give less time to play and more to study. I thought, *Boys are learned and courageous*. So, I would study Greek and practice managing a horse! Then I, too, would be learned and courageous, and my father would be glad.

"I got up early the next morning and ran next door, where I knew that my friend Pastor Hosack would be hoeing his garden. I said, 'Do you like girls better or boys?'

"He answered, 'Why, girls, of course.' Then I said, 'Well, I am a girl and I must learn Greek! Will you please teach me?'

"He found an old, battered Greek grammar he had used himself, and we set to work. I weeded alongside him, and by breakfast-time, I had mastered my first Greek lesson.

"I was so excited and hopeful. It was hard to go back home to the awful gloom at my own house. For Eleazur's funeral, the church bells tolled and tolled. Even now, I shudder at the sound.

"I studied with Pastor Hosack by day and went with Father every evening to the cemetery. When he threw himself upon Eleazur's grave, I leaned against a poplar tree, thinking, might I die, as my brother had? Could learning and courage protect me?

"Pastor Hosack was my great solace. And horseback riding, of course. I rode and rode with the wind, daring myself to go faster and jump higher."

"Four feet high?" Cordelia asked.

"In time," answered Mrs. Stanton. "I drove Pastor Hosack's buggy when he called on parishioners, reciting Greek to him. When he visited our house, I whispered, 'Tell Father how quick I am, how much I've learned!' and he would say what a fine Greek scholar I was. I waited for the words I longed to hear—'She's as good as any boy'—but my father never said them.

"Then Pastor Hosack decided that he had taught me all he knew. A class of boys, all older than I, studied Greek, as well as Latin and mathematics, at the Academy in town. I joined the class, the only girl. People believed that girls' brains were not capable of absorbing anything but simple reading, writing, and arithmetic. After elementary school, they were taught to sew and to paint pretty watercolors.

"The Academy was very hard! I wanted to be taken seriously, as boys were. They stared at me and whispered about me and snickered. But I showed them! I soon ranked second in the class. Two prizes were awarded for excellence at the end of the year. I was determined to win one of them.

"I imagined what would happen. I would run home with my prize in Greek, which no girl had ever won. I would find my father in his office, surrounded by his law books. I would show him my proof of learning. He would not be able to hide his surprise and pleasure. Then he would say, 'Well, a girl *is* as good as a boy after all!'"

"Oh, yes!" Cordelia exclaimed. "And you were courageous, too, jumping on your horse!"

"Finally, Prize Day came. One prize was awarded to a boy. And the other went to—"

"You!" Cordelia cried.

"Yes, to me. I raced home to my father's office, sure that at last he would say that I was as good as any boy. I handed him the prize, a Greek Testament.

"He took it from me. He looked very pleased that I had won it. He asked me some questions about the class. I answered as patiently as I could, since all of my hopes were pinned on hearing those magic words.

He kissed my forehead, sighed, and said, 'Oh, my daughter, you should have been a boy!'"

Cordelia felt her body go limp. "Oh, no!" she said.

"It was a valuable lesson. It taught me to go on fighting. And I have!" Mrs. Stanton replied. "And *you* will, too. You will fight because you are a girl!"

A wagon had drawn up in front of Mrs. Stanton's house. A man got out and rapped on the door.

"We are here to collect voters," said the man.

"The men of the house are away," Mrs. Stanton replied. She glanced at Cordelia. "But I have resided in Tenafly for twelve years. I am three times the legal voting age. And I can read and write. *I* will come and vote."

The men snickered and rolled their eyes. Cordelia was embarrassed for
Mrs. Stanton, but she thought the men were just like Howard, at his worst.

"Cordelia," said Mrs. Stanton, "you follow along on Jule."

Cordelia almost said, "I don't want to go to the poll." But she couldn't
resist riding Jule through town.

"So, Mrs. Stanton," one of the men drawled, "going to make a spectacle
of yourself again?"

They stopped at Watson's Row. "Here is where I pay my taxes," Mrs. Stanton observed. That was a surprise. Cordelia's father paid the taxes in her family, and complained about it.

Men milled around outside. Howard was there, too, with some of his friends.

"Delia!" he called. "Go on home where you belong." She ignored him. But Father might be angry if he knew she was there...

"We have attempted to vote many times over the years," Mrs. Stanton said. "And always our reception is the same. Come inside, Cordelia."

Cordelia had no choice but to follow that command. After all, Jule was Mrs. Stanton's horse!

The poll was filled with men. Mrs. Stanton entered to a buzz of protest. One of her escorts stepped forward and said to the inspectors, "Mrs. Stanton is here, for the purpose of voting." He couldn't keep a straight face.

The inspectors' mouths fell open in mock amazement. One man put his arms around the ballot box and covered the slot with his hand. He said, sarcastically, "Oh, no, madam! Only men are allowed to vote!" The men were all looking. Cordelia was thankful that she was small. She would have preferred to have been invisible.

Mrs. Stanton spoke in ringing tones. "Congress has declared that 'all persons born or naturalized in the United States, and subject to the jurisdiction thereof, are citizens of the United States and of the state wherein they reside' and therefore are entitled to vote. I wish to cast my vote as a *citizen* of the United States."

Two inspectors pulled their hats over their eyes. The one holding the ballot box growled, "It's nothing to do with the Constitution....Women don't vote."

Seeing that she could not put her ballot in the box, Mrs. Stanton flung it at the hand covering the slot, saying, "I have the same right to vote that any man here has."

She threw her magnetic glance around the room and extended
a hand to Cordelia. "The day will come when this girl may vote!"
Two men said, "Hear, hear!"

Cordelia wanted to sink through the floor. She would never vote! How could she endure such shame? How could she *ever* be as brave as Mrs. Stanton!

Outside, Howard and his friends chanted, "No votes for pea-brained females!"
They put their faces up to hers, laughing and mocking.

Something inside Cordelia snapped. She threw herself onto old Jule and gave her a good kick. The boys barely managed to scramble out of the way. She galloped up the street. Was this old horse really worn out? They had to try...

"Jule, let's take that fence!" she cried. "Come on, we can do it!" Jule whinnied, broke into a canter, and sailed over the fence.

Cordelia looked back. It was a good four feet high!

"Bully for you!" shouted Mrs. Stanton. "The old war-horse has fight in her yet!"

Author's Note

Elizabeth Cady Stanton, scholar, author, and mother of seven children, first called for the vote for women at the women's rights convention she organized in Seneca Falls, New York, in 1848. At the time, the notion that women would vote was thought, even by most of those attending the conference, to be a "ridiculous idea." But she persevered. Two years later, she met Susan B. Anthony, and the two fought in devoted partnership for the vote and for equal rights in education, marriage, employment, and government—until Mrs. Stanton died in 1902 at the age of eighty-seven.

Mrs. Stanton was the foremost philosopher of the women's movement and its finest speaker, addressing legislators in state capitals and in Washington, running for Congress in 1866, and publishing a barrage of resolutions, petitions, and articles that kept the issue before the public for fifty years. Remarkably, this brilliant tactician never lost her sense of humor. In 1880, she made the attempt to vote in Tenafly, New Jersey, that is recounted here. After Mrs. Stanton's death, Miss Anthony and many others continued to fight for women's rights. The Nineteenth Amendment, granting women the vote, finally passed in 1920.

Mrs. Stanton believed in equal opportunities of every kind for women: educational, economic, professional, and spiritual. She saw that if women were to free themselves, they would have to change their *own* thinking. They could not let men govern them simply because they were men. She had not wallowed in self-pity when her father devalued her sex, but had instead taken immediate action, developing the qualities that society denied girls. She urged initiative and self-reliance on all women. Her courage, loyalty, wisdom, and zest for life were an abiding inspiration, and remain so today.

For the stories from Mrs. Stanton's life, I drew on biographies by Alma Lutz and Lois Banner, and on Mrs. Stanton's own memoir, *Eighty Years and More*. But Cordelia is a made-up character. She would have been fifty years old in 1920, when she would have cast her first vote, thinking of Mrs. Stanton—and her horse!